Life in ICU

A Medical Thriller Novel

Second Edition

Dr P. Sajeevkumar

emerald

Published in English in India by Emerald
(An Imprint of WINCO BOOKS)
Kottayam, Kerala, India
wincobooks@gmail.com
wincobooks.com

Second Edition 2021
Kindle Edition 2021

LIFE IN ICU
By Dr P. Sajeevkumar

ISBN: 978-93-90759-34-7

Cover Design by Sureshkumar Kuzhimattom
Typesetting and Layout by Winco Publishing Services
Printed and bound in India

India ₹199 | US $9.99

2191431521086***

Chapter 1

RAMAKRISHNAN lay emaciated on bed number one in the ICU. His heart was pulsing its way along a subtle line between life and death. Besides his, a few more hearts were palpitating in the room.

The faces of the patients echoed sadness, but the walls of the ICU were indifferent.

Ramakrishnan's wife stood near to his bed for some time like a bundle of anxiety. Then she moved out. It was on a certain night that he was brought to this hospital. Before that, he had been admitted to a charitable trust hospital in his village. He had been through a heart attack. His heart had lost its rhythm. It would slow down. The sole remedy for him was to install a pacemaker. This hospital does not have that facility. The chief physician had referred him to a distant hospital. But financial vulnerabilities kept him back.

His blood pressure and pumping of the heart were weak. He had breathing trouble. His feet were swollen and urination was not adequate. He altogether could not speak, and the only language of communication was a weak grunt. It was difficult to lie down even. His body was smothered by a phalanx of tubes.

Oxygen tube was inserted into his nostril, drip and nutrients through the blood vessels; another tube was inserted for the removal of urine. On his chest, there were leads for the cardiac monitor. So he was amid a multitude of tubes and wires.

Ramakrishnan had a wife and two daughters. He is almost forty-five and his wife looked as old as he. His eldest daughter has passed the higher secondary examination and the younger one is doing her class ten.

He is a fairly popular electrician in his village. He has been busy with his work. But he loved alcohol more than his family. So liquor shops appropriated a major part of his income. He had been living in a world of blissful oblivion induced by a large variety of drinks.

Though he had been the backbone of the family during his heydays, he had not cared for his family, and now he was helplessly at the dead-end of life. His wife stood outside and brooded over the future of her children.

Ramakrishnan lay on the bed with his eyes glued to the wall. His daughters still hang on to the vague hope that he would recover. They flitted in and out of the hospital for medicines, tea, and porridge. Their mother had long ago given up all hope; she could not even answer the questions of the doctors. She would stand there swallowing her misery, covering herself with a shawl over her saree. Grey tresses were rolling down her lifeless face.

There are two doors to the ICU. One door is for the patients to enter the unit for treatment. And the second door opens to the ward to which the patients will be transferred when they are physically fit for that. Many patients enter through the first door, survive the tremendous moments and move out through the second door back to life. Some others never cross the second door and fade away into eternal silence through an invisible third door. On top of the first door, it is written in red letters: INTENSIVE CORONARY CARE UNIT. Those furious letters ogled at the corridor, casting a spell of fear.

ICU remained indifferent to passaging time and seasons of the year. Chest pain, heart attack, palpitation, weak heart, malfunctioning of the valves – the patients suffered for different reasons. The patients came in one by one and went out one by one. The ICU stood out like an ancient fortress, ready to receive anybody. But this fortress is bereft of the ancient clammy scent of the dead centuries, nor had it the mossy moist walls or rusted metals that weathered the ages.

Its walls were pale green; floors were paved with light blue ceramic tiles. Parapets and deep green curtains separated each cabin of eight beds. Every bed had a unit of the defibrillator, a small cupboard for keeping medicines, a cardiac monitor, a drip unit and a stool to sit on.

The doctor on duty sits at a place where he could observe all the monitors simultaneously. In front of him is an enormous table. Close by, there is a trolley containing injections and medicines. Near the table sat the nurse, ever vigilant. She has an assistant as well. On the iron shelf in the corner, the emergency medical equipment is kept ready. A silent clock frowned down on them to ensure chronological punctuality to all that came to pass in there. The room suffered the chill of the air conditioner.

Outside the room, the sun came and went. Days, lights, and nights took their turns. The wind felt its way in inky darkness. Dewdrops settled on the blades of grass. Outside the unit, seasons of the year marched on, birds warbled in their timeless cadence, flowers bloomed and wilted. In the battle between life and death, the patients were barricaded away from the profuse colours of life.

Doctors, nurses and other service providers came and went turn by turn. The patients also were transferred as soon as they were in a condition to recuperate in the ward close by. Every morning, the unit chief and the assistants would come for the rounds. They would examine the patients and change the medicine regime if necessary.

A cardiac monitor registered the condition of the heart, and it emitted a soft sound. The ICU functioned among the patients, doctors, nurses, and the difficulties of the conditions of the patient.

Ramakrishnan was miserable on the bed. The headrest was lifted. His eyes exuded surprise. Dr Praveen, the postgraduate trainee of the department, visited Ramakrishnan from time to time and his wife would observe the ministrations of the doctor with awful devotion.

She wanted to ask him how her husband was, but she could not. Her tongue remained petrified and unwieldy.

Sr Jessie asked her once, 'Don't you have any relations?'

'None... If something happens to the father of my children, we have only the public road. Will he recover, sister?' she asked, and a scalding drop rolled down her cheek.

'We are doing all that we are worth, have faith,' sister told her.

On the second bed, Kunjikoyammu was kept. This pious Muslim had been here for the last three days. He does not want to remember the excruciating chest pain he had. It was like an enormous boulder pressing down on his chest. He has never had such an experience before.

On the third bed, the patient was one Joseph. He had been here before. On the next one lay Othenan. He is the senior-most in the room. The adjacent bed was occupied by Saradamma. Each bed was like a window possibly opening to life.

Othenan abhorred hospitalisation. Kunjikoyammu was deeply hurt that he could not take part in the memorial service of a Muslim saint, Thakkaley Peermuhammad.

The ICU was followed by the ward, ECG room, echo room, and TMT room, beyond which was the cardiac catheterisation lab followed by the doctor's room. On the ground floor, there were outpatient rooms and a seminar hall.

It was five in the evening and everything was by far peaceful. The ward was almost crowded with visitors. Some of them consoled the patients, some brought food, some others medicine.

When somebody knocked on the door of the ICU, Sr Jessie opened it. It was a bystander.

'Sister, come fast. The patient on bed number ten has blacked out. His bystander is gone out.'

It must be Arumughan, the same story. The sister and her assistant rushed to the bed. Arumughan was writhing. A crowd had gathered around him. Sister felt his pulse. It was too high. Immediately, he was transferred to the ICU. ECG lead was fixed on his chest and connected to the monitor. The emergency bell in the doctor's room came to life.

Urmila, Arumughan's daughter, came to the ward with a glass of tea. Her father was nowhere to be seen. She wondered whether he had gone to the toilet. But he could not go alone in his condition.

'Baby, your father fell unconscious, and he was transferred to the ICU,' said Kanakalatha, wife of the patient Sivarajan. Urmila felt her head spinning and fright roaring up.

* * *

Chapter 2

ARUMUGHAN was a traditional blacksmith by profession. He was around sixty-five. His body had been blackened and desiccated by sitting close to the hearth for most of his life. With the dead weight of his years, Arumughan is not any more dynamic than before.

He was married at twenty. His wife, Karthiyayani was only sixteen. Their first child was born when he was twenty-one. More children were brought to the world in subsequent years – four girls and two boys. One son died young in a bout of diarrhoea. The three elder children were girls, followed by a boy and a girl. The elder daughters were married away in due course. Now they are on their own.

He married away from the girls through restless, hard work. The terrible and exacting years took away his health and vitality progressively. Now he has his son Salgunan and youngest daughter Urmila with him. His wife Karthiyayani had passed away in the previous year by leptospirosis. Salgunan is employed in a private company in town. He has been there for the last many years. His wages are just enough to pull on.

Urmila was apprenticed to a little of tailoring. She manages the house. She had to be married off, and it was a matter of nagging heartburn for her father. She is already twenty-two. Many proposals had come up during the past four years. Nobody disliked her; in fact, she was much better than her prospective suitors in terms of beauty. But Arumughan did not have the wherewithal to marry her away with decent assortments. Even the unemployed and worthless loafers demanded a hefty sum as a dowry. It was not so when his elder daughters have married, demands of the boys were not this high.

It continuously weighed on him that Urmila is still vegetating at home. Karthiyayani had desired to see her daughter living a life of her own. As the youngest daughter, she was her mother's pet.

'What to do, Karthiyayani was unlucky. Otherwise, she wouldn't have left us,' Arumughan used to say.

When the summer festival at Valayanad Bahgavati temple had begun, Karthiyayani went to the temple pond early in the morning to take a holy dip. This resulted in a fatal infection. She developed symptoms of intense fever and shivering. She was properly diagnosed only at the medical college. By that time, it was too late and her liver and kidneys had almost shut down. On the fifth day, she breathed her last, leaving behind many a responsibility.

For a long period, Arumughan had been making and repairing agricultural implements for the farmers of the region. He had a fairly extensive catchment area of trusted clientele. Hence, he was almost always engaged back to back. As old age had overtaken him, Arumughan could not explore away from his hearth in search of additional income.

It happened six weeks ago when he was working on the implements of Krishnan Nair of Manackel family. Heavy pressure in the chest followed a terrible palpitation. He wanted to cry out, his tongue failed him. He could not make out what was happening. He was perspiring profusely, and he swooned. Then his consciousness faded away and nobody noticed.

Urmila called out for him when he failed to turn up for the lunch on time. He could be busy with his work. There was smoke in the smithy. She craned out her young head from the kitchen and found him collapsed on the floor. She darted out crying and tried to shake him up.

'Oh father, oh my god,' she cried out and gasped.

Some neighbours came running to them. They were Chandran, the son-in-law of carpenter Kuttan, Shobhanan the toady tapper, and Narayanan the milking man. All of them together lifted him and put him on the veranda.

Some sprinkled water on his face, some fanned him. He was alive indeed. Around twenty people gathered there. Narayanan checked for his breathing and declared him alive.

'Let us take him to the hospital,' said Chandran.

'We will hail a taxi,' Narayanan and some others rushed out.

The neighbours consoled Urmila. Within half an hour, the taxi driver, Thankappan, appeared beyond the fence in the alleyway. Urmila and her helpers put him in the car, and she put his head on her lap. She piously massaged his chest and abdomen. The car lurched to the hospital. She prayed to the gods for the wellbeing of her father.

He landed up in a bed in the emergency ward. Doctors examined him and demanded ECG. He was given some injections and a blood sample was taken. Once the ECG was examined, he was taken to the ICU by the nursing assistant on a trolley that rolled through the corridor, groaning and croaking protestingly.

His helpless existence dragged on in the ICU for many days. His palpitation would slow down and he would regain consciousness, only for a brief span. Twice he had been transferred to the ward because of improvement, only to be rushed to the ICU again.

Urmila waited in front of the ICU with her sad and reddened eyes. Nobody came out from inside to enlighten her. Her father was all right when she had gone out to fetch a glass of tea for him. Suddenly it happened, whatever it is. She called out to all the known and unknown gods.

Time was dragging on. Her feet were getting weaker. She wanted to meet the doctor or the nurse. She was so anxious. Misery and rage welled up in her and she tried to control herself.

Long later sister opened the door and called out, 'Who is with Arumughan?'

'What is the matter, sister?' Urmila came forward.

'Bring this ampoule for injection,' sister gave her a piece of paper and closed the door in a huff. She flitted down the flight of steps, flaunting the paper. Once on the ground floor, she remembered she had hardly fifty rupees with her. What will be the cost of the medicine? She wondered and anyway she proceeded to the pharmacy.

The medical store was crowded. Her turn came only after ten minutes. She presented the prescription with some trepidation. The pharmacist readjusted his glasses and told her that the medicine was not there. She will have to go to the town.

'But how much will it cost?'

'Around two hundred,' the pharmacist dismissed her in a hurry and turned to the next customer. She felt helpless. Where is the money and who will go to the town? The slurry of events confused her. It occurred to her she could call her brother. She moved to the telephone booth.

* * *

Chapter 3

WHEN Urmila called him on the phone, Salgunan had been supervising the loading of steel bars. His employer sent out somebody to call him to the office. After having attended the land phone, Salgunan stood there, lost in thought.

The hardware business, owned by Idicula Anthappan Lona and his son and now run by Devassy, has a tradition of half a century. Besides steel, they are the wholesale merchants of building materials like cement and paint. They assiduously cultivated their tradition and reliability through honesty, accuracy and true business acumen. They could stand the test of time when many others in the field faded into history. Their business has always been expanding and diversifying. Arumughan and Lonappan had been contemporaries. This factor helped Salgunan find a placement in the firm.

Devassy, the proprietor of the firm, could easily decipher the meaning of Salgunan's silence.

'The phone was from the hospital and you want to go?' he asked.

'Yes.'

'All right, you may go.'

Salgunan still stood there, straining to say something. Devassy looked at him in askance.

'Father is serious! It was my sister who called me. I have to buy some medicines.'

Devassy shook his head with a wry smile.

'You have already taken two months' salary in advance.'

'I know.'

Still, Devassy gave him five hundred rupees. Salgunan took his bag and walked out.

His employer had always been helpful. He had every reason to be grateful. Salgunan had to be on leave very frequently because of his father's illness. The money he had borrowed from Devassy from time to time summed up to two months' salary. Still, he is helpful. Salgunan thanked God, who alone is the refuge.

He boarded the bus to the hospital. Too much time was wasted in the traffic jam. The bus seemed to inch its way, indifferent to the angst of the passengers. Occasionally, he had an urge to flip out of the bus and run to save time.

He entered the casualty ward and ran up the flight of steps. Urmila was waiting for him outside the ICU. He handed the bag to her. She told him about the latest developments. He took the prescription from her and rushed back. He had to reach the town again to get the medicine. The medicine was not available in the medical shops. At last, he got it from a private hospital. He hurried back with the ampoule. During his back-and-forth journey, his mind had been extremely in turmoil.

Inside the ICU, Dr Praveen kept on observing Arumughan. The regular medicines were not responding. His heartbeat was increasing. The graph on the monitor surprised the doctor. The patient's chest showed palpitation. Sr Jessie checked the BP from time to time.

'What should we do, doctor?' sister asked.

'Did they get the ampoule?' the doctor asked back.

'Let me check,' sister went to the door.

'Who is with Arumughan?' she asked.

'Here I am,' Urmila came running to her.

'Where is the ampoule?'

'Wait for a little, sister. My brother will be back shortly with it.'

Sister closed the door.

Salgunan showed up shortly, and the ampoule was passed on. Both brother and sister waited outside.

Arumughan's heart kept on beating like a horse without a bridle. Sister filled in the syringe. The medicine entered the blood vessels of the patient. The doctor stood there watching the monitor.

'I hope this one works,' sister told herself. The doctor watched Arumughan.

The medicine gradually worked on him. The beat was becoming less violent. Perspiration decreased. Arumughan opened his eyes and looked around. He realised he was not in the ward. He recognised the doctor and the nurse. His eyes welled up.

The doctor retired to his table. From there, he could see all the monitors.

Kunjikoyammu would lift his head and look around occasionally. Saradamma was asleep. Joseph understood that something serious was happening around him. Ramakrishnan was still in a critical stage.

'I am tired of this ICU duty. The tragedies and problems of the patients are disheartening. We could do pretty little for them,' sister said.

The doctor was in his chair. He peered into her eyes and said.

'Don't take it like that. At least some of them return to life by our timely intervention. That matters. Death happens because of the gravity of the situation. Don't you know that the first couple of hours are critical of myocardial infarction? Everybody cannot reach the hospital on time and even if they do, all hospitals are not well equipped.'

The doctor said these things to pacify the sister. Yet she was not listening.

'I am not happy here. I am going to request my director of nursing to transfer me to another ward. But she will not be amused. Her long face is a turnoff. I am kept here, as very few have ICU training. I have been stuck here for the last two-and-a-half years.' Sister gave vent to her consternation.

'Don't provoke the director of nursing. All wards have the same story to tell. Patients will come and go. Don't delve deep into their life. Let us do our duty. That will do. Don't venture into the backyard of their lives. That will cause inner turmoil. Stay away from all that,' the doctor advised her.

It was time for duty change. Sister moved to the changing room. The doctor waited for Dr Naushad, who is on night duty.

Urmila and Salgunan waited outside. Silence shrouded them. Ramakrishnan's wife and children also waited outside. There were many more there waiting in trembling hope. ICU was dead to the world outside and its worries. The four walls made all the difference.

* * *

Chapter 4

SISTER Jolly was on night duty. She is one of the few who had some training in ICU management. She loved the job, except for the night duty. She has to strain much during the night duty week. She has two children – four and a half and one and a half years old. At home, she has her husband and his brother. When she is on night duty, they both take care of the children. It was painful. In the evening, when she goes out for night duty, the children will start whimpering. Her husband will have to struggle much to pacify them and distract them from the pains of parting.

After having attended to the patients, the sister called home. The eldest one had already gone to sleep and the younger one was being rocked in the cradle. She felt relaxed and went to her room to have dinner. Nursing assistant Rugmini knocked on the door. Everything was by far all right in the ICU. Sister Resmi from the ward had also been put in the ICU in her absence.

'What is wrong Rugmini?'

'There was a phone call from the casualty. Aishumma is being brought in.'

'All right, I will have my food in a hurry and join you. Please ask Resmi to do what is needed.'

Sister Jolly attacked her food. Aishumma had been in the ICU for two weeks before going home. She had been in the ICU four or five times last year. Every time she came unconscious, stiff.

Aishumma comes with a crowd of children, in-laws, and grandchildren. She has ten children. Three sons are in the Gulf. Two sons are business people in town. All the five daughters have been married away. Each daughter had around five children.

Her husband, Assainar was a timber merchant. He was one of the leading merchants at Kallai. He was the supplier of timber to the barge builders at Beypore, meant for the Arab countries. Youngest son Sameer is now in charge of that venture.

Even today, customers are queuing up at this timber depot. Though he was a prosperous merchant, Assainar had been a polite man. He never showed off. The sheikhs from Arab countries used to visit him at Kozhikode, which added to his reputation in society.

Assainar passed away last year. First, he lost his sound. It was not taken seriously. He had smoked since childhood. After some time, coughs were followed by blood. His people took him to a reputed private hospital. They inserted a tube into his lungs and prognosticated that he had cancer, cancer in the lungs.

After Assainar's death, it was Aishumma's turn. First, it was chest pain, then palpitation and hospitalization. She ended up in ICU many times. Many tests were carried out. Palpitation recurred. Sometimes medicines worked, sometimes she would collapse. The cycle continued.

The assistant brought her to the ICU from the casualty. She was transferred to another trolley in the ICU. The door was closed. Narayanan returned with his trolley and it croaked its way down the corridor.

The doctor examined the patient. Sister arranged the drip; the nursing assistant offered the ECG leads to the sister. She fixed the leads and connected them to the monitor. The doctor checked blood pressure.

'No BP is registered. DC shock is required,' said Dr Naushad.

Sister moved the defibrillator towards the trolley and switched it on to check. It was working. The doctor applied jelly on the paddle and lifted it. Sister and her assistant moved away from the trolley.

'Sister, switch it on. Fifty joules.'

The paddle was placed on Aishumma's chest. The doctor pushed the button. Fifty joules of electricity passed into Aishumma. She jerked her limbs.

The doctor watched the monitor.

'Sister hundred joules, please.'

Sister charged the system again. When a hundred joules was passed, Aishumma cried out 'Allah!'

The monitor showed changes.

'Oh, my mother... Oh Allah,' Aishumma cried aloud.

At two hundred joules, her heartbeat became normal. The monitor showed a normal rhythm. Pulse was once again available on the wrist.

By the time Sister Jolly was back, Aishumma was normal. There was no vacant bed for her. It was transferred Saradamma to the ward close to ICU and to accommodate Aishumma in her place.

Aishumma's children and grandchildren huddled in front of the ICU. Daughters wept and wiped their faces with the tail of the veil. Children played around in their glittery garments and jingling bangles.

Then Sameer noticed somebody vaguely familiar. It was Urmila sitting on the bench, eyes downcast. Last time also he had met Urmila. He went to her. Discerning the language of his feet, she raised her head. Seeing him, her face brightened up.

'We brought our mother again,' he said.

'Father is still here. He never went back,' she said.

'So many days!'

'He was transferred to the ward twice. Now it is back to square one.'

He watched the deep shade of melancholy spreading on her youthful face. In the meantime, Sister Jolly opened the door.

'Sister, how is our mother,' one woman asked.

'She is better. Don't crowd here. Please move away,' sister said with a tinge of impatience. Urmila went to Sister Jolly.

'Sister, how is our father?'

'You mean Arumughan? He is better now.'

Sister went out. Urmila felt quite relieved. Sameer herded the women and children away as night was thickening and the children may doze off after a while. Sameer went out in search of a room in the nearby lodges. They heard a siren in front of the casualty. An ambulance screeched in with a glaring red beacon.

* * *

Chapter 5

DR Praveen was in the ICU in the afternoon. He felt a bit drowsy after lunch. The air-conditioned environment in the ICU was welcome for a nap. He dozed away for almost ten minutes. Then Vilasini barged in, pushing open the door. The doctor opened his eyes. Giving him a sweet smile, she went to the sisters' room in the corner of the ICU.

She was the secretary to the professor of the cardiology department. She had been in charge of dealing with the matters about the department and the office, files of the doctors, encashing the salary bills at the treasury, etc. In the beginning, she had worked as a nursing assistant as well. Later on, taking an in-service test, she became LD Clerk. She had retired from service four years back. Still, she continues on daily wages. She knows everything about the nurses, PG trainees, unit chiefs of the cardiology department, their assistants and other staff.

Though she was almost sixty, Vilasini was as dynamic as a young lady. Her artificial teeth reduced her age. She puts on soft coloured sarees. There is an ear of basil in her oily hair. A smear of sandal paste on her forehead and a red dot in the middle are her trademarks.

She has the freedom to visit ICU. She comes and goes at will. As soon as the professor's office is closed at noon, she retires to the sister's room. Most of the telephone calls to the ICU in the afternoon will be for her. Thus, she beamed in the ICU, almost like a professor. In the medical college office, she had strong connections. She could chase the files where the doctors failed. Also, she could intervene in the treatment matters of the office staff.

She was always eager to help others. She cared for all. There was not a trace of snobbery. She trusted in the warmth of friendship and the happiness of helping others. She believed that happiness in life is the happiness of togetherness.

After a few minutes, she reappeared from the sisters' room. She settled on a chair close to the doctor.

Sister Amala was also with her. Amala went to the ward.

'This morning when I came to the office, you were arguing with the professor. What was that for?' she asked.

'Oh, it was nothing. I had asked for leave. He denied it. I need to go on leave. I want to see my firstborn. Now he has vetoed it.'

'You must give us a treat, now that you are a father.'

'Let me see him first. The treat will follow.'

'It is all right. I was just kidding. It is a wonderful thing to have a child, especially when husband and wife are in different places. Our Jessie sister is miserable. Poor thing! They have been married for eight years and have not had a child yet. Her husband was in Bombay. She used to stay with him for three months every year. But nothing happened. Then he resigned from his job and came back home to be together. Still, it is all the same. They have consulted all the doctors and professors here. Many tests were conducted. Many medicines were tried. Sister has given up hope. Yes, having a child is an important thing in life.'

Vilasini continued her typical analysis of current events. The doctor was mesmerised by her eloquence. She was like that. She needed somebody to listen to her. She was oblivious to the time consciousness of others. Still, nobody disliked her.

'Doctor, please come,' sister called out from Ramakrishnan's bed.

The doctor rushed to the spot.

'There is no blood pressure now,' she said.

The doctor examined the patient. There was only a soft murmur from him and there was no pulse. The body had become stiff. But the monitor registered a heartbeat. The doctor gave some instructions to the sister and moved to the door. Opening the door, he called out, 'Who is with Ramakrishnan?'

'What happened doctor?'

Mother and daughters came towards him. They had been squatting on the floor, tired and woebegone.

'Ramakrishnnan is in a critical condition. You may see him one by one. Do not cry or disturb the patients. If you want to inform somebody, do it soon.'

The mother and children were stunned by the information. They said nothing. They did not even cry. Doctors went back to the ICU as if he had done his duty. Sister gave an injection for Ramakrishnan. The doctor was at his table. Then he heard a big sound from the fourth bed. Othenan was roaring he had flung away his dhoti and was trying to leap out of the bed.

'It is so hot. I need a dip in the temple pond.' He got up from the bed. The walls became a silent witness to his incoherence.

Doctor, sister and nursing assistant seized him immediately. Even at eighty-three, his muscles were still healthy. He was almost six feet tall and an imposing figure and his voice were imperious.

He was the oracle at Muchilot Bhagavati Temple. He did not like hospital life. He was brought to the hospital when he fell unconscious on the temple premises. On the same day, he was transferred to the ICU. He had two sons with him, both in their late fifties. But Othenan looked healthier than them. And he was even more handsome.

For a couple of days, Othenan had been delirious.

'I must go. I must put on the jingles of the goddess. A dip in the temple pond will cure everything. Why should you keep me here?'

He continued to banter. The doctor and others struggled to calm him down. The nursing assistant covered his nudity with his flung dhoti. His son was called in. Othenan kept on mumbling.

'First, you get well, old man. Then you can have your holy dip,' the doctor said.

The commotion alerted everybody in the ICU. But nobody could understand anything properly.

* * *

Chapter 6

RAMAKRISHNAN remained like that for many more hours. The doctor knew that he was sinking and that it was impossible to bring him back to the living world. But he was not yet dead. His wife and children stood close to him for some time and sighed. They did not cry.

They had nobody to inform. Somebody from Sreeramakrishna Ashram had helped them financially. Ramakrishnan's daughters called him uncle. The same man had come in the morning to discuss Ramakrishnan with the doctors.

'We are doing for him what we can. Find your consolation in that, baby. Nothing is in our hands. The one in the heavens decides it all. We are pawns in his hands. Watch and pray. That is all,' he had counselled the elder girl when he was going back.

As Dr Praveen was on leave, Dr Naushad was on duty. The eerie drizzling begun in the evening had graduated to a roaring rain at night. A chilly wind was sweeping outside. Dr Naushad had come for duty with a good mind to take a nap.

Aishumma was a little better. So was Arumughan. Outside the door, Aishumma's family members huddled up. Nobody in the team had gone back. They waited on the veranda. Turn by turn, they took permission to visit Aishumma. They would give her coffee and rice porridge. Twice a day, they would sit in a circle on the veranda and eat biryani or ghee rice. At that time, the veranda would be saturated with the powerful aroma of Islamic food. At night, women and children would stay in the lodge outside. It was Sameer's turn to wait on Aishumma.

Arumughan's condition was under control. Salgunan had been going to work for the last three days. Urmila stayed in the hospital. Every evening, Salgunan would turn up.

Most often, Sameer and Urmila would go out for food together. They had become acquaintances when Aishumma was brought there last time. Sameer had volunteered to buy the medicines prescribed for Arumughan for her. Sometimes he would bring food as well. When he was with her, Urmila experienced happiness and confidence. She could forget the monotony and the sorrows of the hospital life. Urmila was on a chair on the veranda. Ramakrishnan's wife and children were waiting a little away. Their eyes were red and swollen.

'Here is some lemon juice. Have a sip, please,' Sameer offered a PET bottle to Urmila. She refused it shaking her head.

'Please have a little,' he insisted.

Yielding to his pressures, she gulped a little of the drink. Then they killed time talking about sundry little things. He exuded the scent of attar. She had noticed that he had distinct scents every day. He played on the cell phone. She was feeling sleepy. When she said that she was going to the ward, he showed her the cell phone.

'Look at this, please,' he said.

She strained her face to look into the phone. Her photo was there. He pressed another button and another photograph of hers appeared.

'How could you do that?' she asked wonderstruck.

'This has a built-in camera. It was brought from abroad. I took the photos for the fun of it.'

She was alarmed. Still, she walked away. He watched her going away. Her curvaceous body and cute face fascinated him.

It was midnight. Dr Naushad had slept away. Somebody rang the emergency bell. The doctor got up with a start and went to the ICU.

'The monitor is flat,' the sister attending on Ramakrishnan said. She waited for further instructions from the doctor. The doctor tried to feel his pulse. Then he put on the stethoscope and examined him. After a couple of minutes, the doctor said, 'Do nothing.'

For some time, he had been travelling on the subtle line between life and death. Now the journey draws to an end. There is nothing more to do. That is better. Medicine is of no use when death is invincible and inevitable. Further interventions will not serve any purpose. The doctor told himself. He went to his table and picked up Ramakrishnan's case sheet and wrote.

'Sister, inform his relatives, please,' he said.

Sister removed the drip unit and opened the door. She called the elder daughter and passed the information. The reaction was a scream. The scream reverberated across the hospital. His wife and younger daughter also followed the suit.

They tried to crash into the ICU. Some people forcefully restrained them. Then they rolled on the floor and cried. Witnessing that tears welled up in the eyes of the onlookers. Alerted by the commotion, many more came to the veranda from the ward. Shortly, a crowd was formed there. They had been observing the mother and children for the past few days.

Who will protect this poor family? They wondered. The mother and children were at a loss. They had nobody to turn to. Then the elder daughter remembered the uncle at Ramakrishna Ashram. He had given the phone number.

Sameer and some others were preparing to do something for the bereaved family. Sister called the mother in to fill in a form. Elder daughter pulled out a small shabby book from inside her bag and searched for the phone number.

'Give me the phone number. I will call him over the phone. You just wait here,' Urmila volunteered.

'Just pass this information,' the girl said, almost like a whisper. The daughters embraced and the elder one wiped the tears of the younger.

When Urmila was going down the steps with the phone number, Sameer joined her.

'Don't go alone. I will come with you,' said Sameer.

They went out through the casualty to the telephone booth. Outside, it was like a day with all the neon bulbs on. The booth was deserted. She dialled the number and passed the message. The man at the other end listened to the message with gentleness. It was informed that the uncle would reach the hospital immediately. He would bring the ambulance also to take home the dead body.

'That is good. That will be a great help for that mother and children. They cannot arrange an ambulance themselves,' Urmila told Sameer.

They don't have money; I guess. I will give you some money. Can you give it to the girls?' Sameer asked on the way back.

'Oh yes, with pleasure.'

Sameer pulled out a leather purse from his jeans pocket and gave her five hundred rupees. She accepted it and put it in her money purse.

From the casualty, they walked up the steps. The corridor on the first floor was deserted. The light was feverish and dim. The silence was heavy. At the end of the corridor, there was a flight of steps to the ICU block. Silence enveloped both of them. Suddenly, the power supply went. It was pitched darkness. On an impulse, she held Sameer's hand. They stood there. In that darkness, lightning of excitement streaked through him. He held her close. Then he planted passionate kisses on her cheeks and luscious lips. She couldn't say anything. She did not even understand what was happening. Blood raged through her limbs. Her body was afire. A strange feeling devoured her. Her arms held him close. For a moment, the world ceased to exist. Then her money purse slipped down. Suddenly, she woke up to reality.

‘What is this Sameer? Why did you do this to me?’

He kissed her again and said, ‘I wanted it. I like you, I love you.’

* * *

Chapter 7

IT has been many days since Saradamma was transferred to the ward. She was feeling better. But not yet completely recovered. The medications will have to continue. Otherwise, chest pain and breathing problems will recur.

Saradamma is a spinster and lives alone. Her sister's children would occasionally help her. The hospital also took turns looking after her. As they were manual labourers, they would lose a day's wage when they were with Saradamma. Still, they looked after her.

Othenan was a little better. After being transferred to the ward, the doctor had given sleeping pills for a couple of days. He had not yet understood why he was detained in the hospital now that he was healthy, even at eighty-three. It is rumoured that his ancestors were from the legendary family of Thacholy. He is a fairly known martial artist. For the last three decades, he had been the oracle at Muchilot Bhagavathi temple. His life was dedicated to the goddess. Hence, a life outside the temple premises was unbearable to him. Early in the morning, he would get up and do his exercises. Then a holy bath in the temple pond will follow. By the time the priest comes, Othenan will wait under the peepul tree. He would do sundry chores in the temple. At eight-thirty he would be back at home to have his regular breakfast of two baked papads, steaming rice porridge and pickle made of tender mangoes. Long back, he used to go for manual labour. Later, he stopped it. At noon, he would have his lunch and siesta. At five, he takes a bath and goes to the temple. At eight, he returns for dinner made of rice porridge. At ten, he goes to bed. The doctors have incarcerated such a punctual man. It was beyond his comprehension.

Dr Ramdas, who is the chief of unit two, discharged five patients during his rounds in the morning. Saradamma and Othenan were among them. Othenan felt as if he was coming out of the jail. However, Saradamma loved hospital life. At home, she will be alone. In the hospital, there are people around. Human presence gave her confidence. However, the hospital cannot be an orphanage.

'Don't stop the medicines. Come to the OP after a month,' the doctor told Saradamma. Chief told Dr Praveen that Arumughan could be transferred to the ward on the coming day. His condition was satisfactory.

Urmila had been in a strange mood for many days. She could not concentrate. Mind was like a tree twirled and battered in the hoary wind. Thoughts flitted through the boughs of her mind. She could not properly attend to her father. She forgot to buy the medicines many times. Sister had reprimanded her once. The event that happened that night haunted her. She kept on regurgitating it. What happened in the darkness? Sameer was taken to be a gentleman. He had brought her into the warmth of his embrace. She experienced the sweetness of his lips. The heady natural musk of his mixed with exotic scent still lingers in her nostrils. Did she provoke him when she held his hand in the darkness? Or did he purposely do it to molest her modesty? She had yielded to the temptation for a moment. She had embraced him. Who is to be blamed?

She analysed it from various angles. The words of Sameer echoed in her ears, 'I like you, I love you.'

Does he love her? Could that be true?

She had been shying away from him for the last many days. Shame and fright-filled her. But he was all the same. He used to smile at her as usual. In the evening, he saw her coming back with food.

'Just a minute. Are you angry with me?'

She glued her eyes on the ground and walked on.

'I know I was wrong. It just happened. It was an impulse. What misguided me? Mind or body. I know not. Still, I love you,' he said.

She said nothing. What can she say – to love her or not to love her?

'Tell me something,' he said. He blamed himself for looking at the confusion on her face. He cursed himself. He knew he was wrong. She or anybody else would take him to be a beast.

'Your silence is killing me, at least scold me,' he said.

His words pierced her. Tears rolled down. She wiped her tears and said, 'What can I say? Why should I scold you?'

She disappeared from the scene. Sr Jessie, who came that way, looked at them. Sameer stood there watching Urmila going away.

* * *

Chapter 8

ARUMUGHAN spent his days in the ward. He felt much better. He had spent a long period in the hospital. The hospitalisation this time was, however, unexpected. His homestead must be in disarray. He had remained insulated from the world outside. He was eager to go home.

'Did the doctor say anything about discharge?' he asked Urmila in the evening.

'No.'

'Let him stay in the hospital until the doctor permits him to go home. Otherwise, we will be in trouble again,' Salgunan told her.

Every day of their father being in the hospital was a drain on him. His debts were accumulating. That does not matter. He would rather wait until his father was formally discharged.

Salgunan sat close to his father. Arumughan asked him about the news outside. Has the plaster been removed from the arms of Kunjukrishnan the mason? Has mail deliverer Kanaran finished his house construction? When the questions found no end,

Salgunan wanted to escape. His father is very anxious about the world outside the moment he feels a little better.

When Salgunan was going out, Urmila accompanied him with the tiffin carrier.

'You have suffered a great deal, haven't you?' he asked her on the way to the canteen.

'No chance. This is not suffering. I have nothing else to do.'

'Father has many more daughters elder than you. They could come and stay, at least they could enquire about his condition by visiting us once in a while. They have their husbands and children, and father is not their concern.'

'It doesn't matter. I am not unhappy. No need for anybody to relieve me. I hope things do not get worse,' Urmila said.

From the canteen, he walked to the exit gate and she to the ward. Then strange thoughts crowded her mind. Why was she not speaking to Sameer? He had confessed everything. Then why was she ignoring him? It must hurt him. Nobody else had seen what had happened between them on that night. She would live her days away as if it never happened. She would bury it all in the past and be with him as before. That is better. Wild thoughts will only hurt the mind.

Aishumma was still in the ICU. She was not improving. This time, her disease defied the treatment. She had been delirious for the last two days. In the evening, she told the doctor that it was too hot and that the fan was not good. Everybody suppressed laughter.

'The fan is at full speed and the AC is on. Still, is it hot?' the doctor joked.

'Yes, it is boiling, and the fan is not enough.'

'The fan is failing because you have eaten up all the electricity. You were given shock treatment many times,' the doctor said in a light vein and stood near her for some time more. Then, with a smile, he moved to the next bed.

As it was evening, there were many visitors on the ward and veranda. When Urmila was returning to the ward, she met Sameer outside the ICU. He smiled at her. Her eyes bloomed at his smile. Her cheeks blushed. Urmila bent her head and walked to the ward. At every bedside, there were three or four visitors. Arumughan sat on the bed. He had been instructed not to talk much. He was to lie down, sit up and go to the toilet with the help of an assistant.

'Give me some water,' Arumughan said to Urmila.

She offered him a glass of water and watched him drink it.

'Are you ready for the rice porridge?' she asked.

'No, not yet.'

'Then I will come back shortly. I will be close by,' she walked out of the ward. She looked for Sameer outside the ICU. He was there. He stood up and came to her. She strolled.

'How is your mother,' she asked.

'I cannot say. Doctors say that things are not promising.' his sound seemed weak. He sat on a bench in the corridor.

'Could you please sit with me on this bench for a minute or two?' he pleaded.

She could not resist him. People were rushing back and forth. Everybody was busy. Nobody had time for anybody else. After a brief spell of silence, he asked, 'Are you still angry with me?'

'Yes.'

They talked for some time, taking it out of the mind. The tension was eased out by and by.

Sr Jessie wanted to meet the director of nursing. She needed a transfer from the ICU. Sr. Jessie was good at the job. Also, she knew how to deal with the patients and their people. Her problem was that she had none to confide in. She was unhappy with her barren life.

She was troubled because her husband could not find a suitable placement after coming back from Bombay.

She was happy in the presence of Dr Praveen. He had advised her not to seek a transfer from the ICU. Still, she was determined. She was tired of ICU duty. There was no space for relaxation. She even detested the profession she had chosen. Tomorrow she would meet the director of nursing. Nobody else would do that for her.

The head nurse in charge of ICU, Santhakumari, was coming to ICU from casualty. In the crowd, she observed Urmila and Sameer on the bench. Something was wrong. Sister could make it out.

Her intuitions had never gone amiss. She had been in the profession for thirty years. She had met thousands of patients, different people with different family backgrounds. She had witnessed many emotional situations. Hence, she could easily read out the inner climate of the people she came across.

* * *

Chapter 9

DR. Praveen had a busy day. From eight in the morning, he was at the OP department. In the beginning, the chief and one assistant professor were in the OP with him. After one hour, the assistant professor went for the rounds. After a while, the chief also made himself scarce, claiming that he needed tea. After having examined everybody in the OP department, Dr Praveen went to the echo centre. The professor could do echo tests only on twelve patients per day. But many more will come with prescriptions got from the unit chiefs at home. They could spoil his career. Hence, he had to oblige the additional patients too. When he came out of the echo room, it was already two o'clock. He was hungry and had a splitting headache. He did not even have the regular tea at ten. Hence, he straight went to the canteen for lunch.

While coming back, he met Dr Naushad. Then only he was informed that it was his turn to present a case for the coming day's clinical discussion. That deepened his headache. Not willing to do anything for a while, he retreated to the comfort of the ICU. The air conditioner felt good for him.

Sr Jessie was giving midday medicines. Aishumma was not improving. Her heartbeat was erratic. She was given electric shock four times already. Her daughters, grandchildren and Sameer were always outside the door.

Dr Praveen was toying with the prospect of selecting the patient Rema in the ward for the prospective discussion. Rema's condition was satisfactory. He examined Rema thoroughly in the ward. He wanted to note down the entire case history. Sr Jessie came to his table.

'Doctor, I am going to take the USMLE exam this time.'

'That is wonderful. Are you tired of treating Indians?'

'No doctor. If I pass the test, I could go out and see unseen lands. Different circumstances, different people, different styles. We will get a family visa and we could be together.'

'In short, it is an infatuation for the white-skinned people, is it not?' the doctor taunted her.

'I am telling you the truth, doctor. I have joined a coaching centre in town. It will last for two months.'

'Well, well. Please tell Rema and the bystander to come to the examination room at five.'

'Yes doctor,' she went to the ward. Dr Praveen flipped over the case sheets in the ICU. He compared the temporal variation of the ECG and noted down the inferences. The patients were Aishumma, Kunjuraman, Abdulla, Narayanan, Varghese, and others.

Vilasini stormed into the ICU. She smiled at the doctor and examined the postal goods on the table.

'I was checking whether payslip for Dr Shyam had come,' she told the doctor.

She put the file on the table and went to the sister's room. After a few minutes, she came out with her bag as fast as an arrow.

Sister came to the ICU from the ward and glanced over at the cardiac monitors. The monitors registered normal rhythms.

'I have told Rema. The bystander is her mother-in-law. She is an impossible woman.'

'OK,' the doctor said.

'Do you know her story, doctor? She has been coming to the hospital for the last two years on and off.'

'Tell me more,' he encouraged her. Then she told the entire story.

Rema's parents had passed away in her childhood. She has an elder sister. She and her family do not care for Rema. Rema was brought up by an aunt, almost like her own daughter. Rema studied up to class eight. Then she dropped out and supported her aunt at home. Later on, she became a manual labourer. She worked at the flour mill, became a gardener and even a seamstress at various stages.

When she was twenty, marriage proposals trickled in. One proposal was from a young man called Damu. He was a hard-working man. She had seen him before. Aunt liked that proposal. Damu had his mother only. She also was a labourer. Both families fixed the marriage. Aunt gave fifteen thousand rupees and eighty grams of gold ornaments for the marriage.

On the first night itself, Rema had breathing trouble when she reached Damu's house. She was taken to the nearest doctor. From that night onwards, she coughed. The moment she lies down cough will smother her. The first night itself was a nightmare. Damu consoled her. She was again taken to the doctor. Still, the cough did not subside.

One week came to pass. Every night was hard. Besides cough, she had breathing trouble. Two years back when she was at the flour mill, she had breathing problems. A brief treatment cured it. Taking pity on the suffering of Rema, Damu's mother took her to the astrologer Balapanicker who lived close to the local administration office. He studied the position of the stars and said that the time was not good for her. He gave her a talisman.

A talisman was tied on her arm and waist. Four more days passed. There was no respite at night still. Her suffering was only exacerbated. From the first day of his marriage, Damu's duty was to massage her back and make black tea for her. Rema felt sorry for him. His mother was unhappy about the situation.

'My child was tricked into marrying a sick woman. She was sick from birth and they did not divulge the truth.'

The next day, they went to the astrologer again. He was asked to suggest a good doctor. The astrologer suggested a private hospital in which he had a share. That night, Rema vomited. Her face and feet were swollen, and she did not have the energy to walk.

Damu and his mother took her to the hospital in a three-wheeler. On the way, she collapsed. This happened near the doctor's house, whom they had consulted before. Damu took her to the same doctor. His mother was not happy with that volte-face.

The doctor examined her and gave two injections. Then she was referred to the medical college.

'It is a case of heart failure. Hurry her to the medical college,' he said.

That is how she reached medical college. She was in the ward for few days. Then she was transferred to the cardiology ward. After the echo test, it was diagnosed to be cardiomyopathy.

It is a reasonless disease that medicine can not cure completely. Death can overtake her. Many times she had been hospitalised during the past two years.

* * *

Chapter 10

IN the morning when the unit chief came for the rounds, Aishumma's condition had deteriorated. Her memory was blurred and her blood pressure was precariously low. The medicines were not responding. The chief prescribed some new medicines. Dr Praveen noted them in the case sheet and gave instructions to the sister.

'Inform the relatives of hers. I think she will not overcome this time,' the chief said before moving to the next bed. Dr Praveen remained in the ICU.

Head nurse Santhakumari walked into the ward after the rounds in the ICU. She assessed the hygiene and condition of the beds in the ward. On the way back, she noticed Urmila. She was coming back to the ward after some shopping. The head nurse asked her to come and meet her after going to the ward.

Urmila was flabbergasted. What could be the matter? She went to the ward immediately and placed the purchase on the table. Then she went to the room of the head nurse with the permission of her father. She stood hesitantly at the door.

'Do come in,' said the head nurse.

She stepped inside. The head nurse observed her through the thick glasses. She was serious. After closing and setting aside the duty book, she asked how her father was.

'Little better, sister.'

'Do you know why I wanted to meet you?'

'No, sister.'

'No, you will understand nothing. That is why I called you. I have been in this profession for the last thirty years. I have worked in many hospitals in different places and met many people. I can understand their psychology. There was one Chandrika in the dermatology ward five years back. She was always sick and bedridden for one and a half years. Doctors brought medicines even from foreign countries to treat her. She had a daughter just like you. This girl developed a discrete relationship with one supplier in the canteen. I advised her. She said that it was like her age. I don't want a justification like that from you. It is not good for you to walk and talk with that young man. Better stop it for your good.'

Urmila stood there, petrified. Does she allude to the matter with Sameer? But there is nothing between her and Sameer. Could that be something else? Urmila could not open her mouth.

'You may go now,' sister told her.

Urmila's eyes were wet. She went to the ward, wiping her tears.

Dr Praveen went to Aishumma's bedtime and again. The graph was flattening on the monitor. Her pulse was diminishing. Breathing was difficult.

'Doctor, should we use the defibrillator?' sister asked with some energy.

'No, sister.'

Let her have some peace at the end of the journey. There is no need to make it terrible with an electric shock. He reasoned.

Outside, Aishumma's children waited in tears. They chorused, 'Allah, Allah.' Sameer stood close to the door. To date, his mother used to come out of the ICU cured. It pained him that the situation was different this time.

Aishumma passed into silence after a while. One more heart snapped its link with the world and migrated into the invisible. The doctor opened the door and passed the information to Sameer. His eyes became wet. Seeing that, Aishumma's daughters cried aloud. Their cries crossed the boundaries of the corridor.

The cries and screams continued for some time. Then the men herded the women to the ground floor. The doctor prepared the death report of Aishumma. Shortly, the body was covered with white clothes and taken out. The trolley creaked its way along the corridor. On the way, people gazed at the trolley. Sameer walked ahead, swallowing his sorrow. An ambulance was waiting outside.

Dr Praveen remained in the ICU. Vilasini came to visit him.

'Is that Muslim lady dead?' she asked. Then she looked at the vacant bed. The walls of the ICU were indifferent.

'Do you know the story of bed number one and three,' Vilasini asked.

'What story?'

Vilasini told another story from her invisible history book. Sr Jessie went to her room as she had heard the story before.

'It happened a quarter of a century back. I had served only for three years. One day in the evening, the then minister K. G. Kurup and two of his attendants came to meet his mother on bed number one. The doctor on duty was from Karnataka state. He was very strict but committed to the job. The doctor did not know that the visitor was a minister. He got angry when the minister opened the door of the ICU. He shouted at them to get out. Ignoring him, the minister moved ahead. The doctor shouted to get out and seized the minster's collar, which ensued a fisticuff. The minister fell. The doctor's reaction was unexpected. Nobody expected it. The minister's followers got furious with the doctor.

The doctor understood nothing still. The sisters and hospital staff assembled there. The doctor was shattered and embarrassed when he came to know that it was a minister. He cried. Seeing him crying, the minister also cried. The doctor sought forgiveness. The minister said that it was his fault. He should not have come unannounced. It took some time for the dust to settle. Then the minister enquired into the condition of his mother on bed number one.

The developments on that day inflicted much mental tension on the minister. Within three days, he was brought to the ICU on a trolley. He was on bed number three. His mother was still on bed number one. The minister breathed his last after one week.

* * *

Chapter 11

AROUND 3 o'clock, Dr Praveen was summoned to the medical ICU. The pulse of a patient there had dangerously decreased. On that day, Sister Jolly was on duty in the cardiology ICU. She told him about this issue in the medical ICU. Shortly, he went to the medical ICU.

In the medical ICU, all the beds were occupied. The patient in question was suffering from fever and hepatitis. The liver and kidneys were out of order. One round of dialysis was over already. His heart was in disorder. It was too risky to remove him from another ICU. The doctor studied the case and gave appropriate instructions.

On the way back, he went to the milk booth near the casualty to have a cup of tea. The roaring business was going on there. The chief merchandises were coffee, tea, snacks and buttermilk. It was open round the clock. After tea, he sauntered his way to the casualty. It was unusually crowded.

Accidentally, he noticed Sr Jessie seated in a chair. Her husband stood close by. Sr Jessie was seated, supporting her arms on the knees. Her face was faded, and she had lost her original charm. Dr Praveen went to her. Sr Jessie could not see him or recognise him. He asked her husband what had happened.

'She had gone to bed after dinner last night. She did not get up even at seven in the morning. I tried to wake her up, and she gestured she had a headache. Then I left her to sleep. I forced her to get up at twelve. But she could not stand on her feet. After washing her face, I served her tea. Again, she went to bed. Then I hailed a taxi and brought her here. It is almost half an hour. Because of the rush doctors could not attend to us.' Her husband told the entire story in one breath. There was anxiety on his face.

'Don't worry. Let us take her upstairs. I will take care of her,' Dr Praveen told him.

He realised that Sr Jessie was deep asleep. From casualty, he made a phone call to the cardiology ICU. He asked nursing assistant Kumaran to bring a wheelchair to the casualty. Sister Jolly thought it was for some stranger.

Another fifteen minutes passed before Kumaran appeared with the wheelchair. Dr Praveen was standing near Sr Jessie and her husband.

'What happened to the sister?' Kumaran was alarmed.

'Take her to the ICU. It is nothing serious,' said Dr Praveen. Kumaran took Jessie in a hurry across the corridor. Dr Praveen asked him to lay Jessie in the observation room next to the cardiology catheterisation lab. Sister Jolly and Vilasini came running. Jessie's husband waited outside with a disturbed mind. The doctor called her. She was very drowsy. She could not open her eyes. After checking BP and pulse, he asked them to start the drip. Glucose entered her bloodstream. After five minutes, Jessie opened her eyes. She looked around and recognised the doctor, Jolly and Vilasini.

Dr Praveen had some doubts. Jessie looked at everybody. Where was she? How could she reach there? She did not know. Dr Praveen asked the women to stay out for a while. Then he went closer to Jessie and examined her eyes. There were teardrops gathered in the corners.

'Did you take any tablets in excess?' Dr Praveen asked.

She did not speak out for some time. Tears rolled down her cheeks.

'Please tell me the truth,' the doctor said.

'Yes,' she nodded.

'What did you take?'

'Alprazolam, ten tablets, last night.'

It was an answer he had been waiting for. But what could be the motivation for that? He could not understand. She seemed to have some mental tension. Let this be a secret. People will fabricate stories if such a suicide attempt comes to the open. It will affect her reputation. She has many more years of professional life.

The doctor went outside. He asked certain questions to her husband and consoled him. Then he called Vilasini and went inside. He whispered in her ear, 'This is a secret. Sister had excess tablets. Please give her a stomach wash.'

Vilasini stared at the doctor, unable to believe what she had heard. Then she looked at Jessie. She found some mysteries looming there. Why was the doctor taking the risk? If she dies doctor will be held responsible. The hullabaloos thereof will be contagious and unmanageable. Vilasini remained in her reverie for some time. Then she went out.

She brought back the tube and accessories for the stomach wash. They closed the door from inside. Doctor and Vilasini carried out the stomach wash. Nobody came to know about this. Jessie's husband waited outside innocently.

Vilasini and the doctor stood close to her. After some time, Jessie talked.

'Sorry, doctor.'

She looked at him, and he patted her hand.

'Nobody knows about this. Let this remain a secret.' Vilasini caressed her hair and said. Her drip was finished in the meantime. Around eight o'clock, she expressed her desire to go back home. The doctor permitted her to do so.

'Don't repeat this foolishness. Nobody knows about this, not even your husband. It will be a humiliation to you if people came to know. You have many more years of professional life. After a couple of days, take psychology counselling. I will guide you. Now go home and relax.'

Jessie and her husband went back home. That night, Dr Praveen could not sleep.

* * *

Chapter 12

Every Wednesday there is an academic programme symposium. It usually begins at 8:15 in the morning. Dr Praveen walked briskly from his hostel to the hospital. Today's presentation was that of Dr Vineeth. Dr Praveen and Dr Naushad are from the examination going batch and hence it was their duty to arrange everything. He was a little late. He hurried across the hospital compound, ran up the staircase and entered the hall, puffing and panting. He was lucky; the professor had not come yet. To his surprise, the other chiefs also were not there. It was quite unusual.

'What happened? Has the programme been postponed?' Dr Praveen asked Dr Naushad.

'Today's programme has been cancelled. The professor is furious. Yesterday, one patient died. He was the neighbour of Prof. Krishnan of the surgery department. Prof. Krishnan accused our professor that the death happened because of the delay in the blood transfusion. The professor is questioning us all. You are also asked to meet him.' Dr Naushad said.

The news outraged Dr Praveen. Blood rushed to his face. His face became beet red.

'Who said it was because of the delay in blood transfusion? Let Prof. Krishnan go to hell. We should not be carried away by his nonsense. You know the diagnosis of the patient in question. It was alcoholic liver disease, portal hypertension and unstable angina. Yesterday he had haematemesis and chest pain. He was referred to gastroenterology as a surgery casualty. No bed was vacant there. Then the patient's relations called Prof. Krishnan on the phone. Prof. Krishnan called our second chief and requested the patient to be admitted to the cardiology ICU as he had chest pain. The unit chief called me on the phone and asked me to admit the patient to the ward. Prof. Krishnan also was with the patient. I admitted him to the ICU itself, as Prof. Krishnan was with him. His ECG was normal. He vomited blood once. Immediately, I had planned for a blood transfusion. By the time my duty was over, blood was entering his system. Dr Vineeth says that later on, he collapsed. What more can we do? Professor has no reason to be furious. I would rather meet the professor after discussing this with the unit chief.'

Dr Praveen went to the OP section and met Dr Sudhakara Menon, chief of unit two. Once the patient who was consulting him was dismissed, Dr Praveen told the entire story. Dr Menon consoled him. We did nothing wrong. Our fault is that we tried to help them. Dr Menon asked him to meet the professor as well.

Professor's door was half-closed. When he entered the room, the professor was found deeply engrossed in a thick book. He lifted his head now that Dr Praveen was there.

'Sir, you wanted me to meet you.'

'Yes, what happened yesterday?'

Dr Praveen explained his side of the story.

Professor listened to the last and said that if one of his students was blamed, it was tantamount to blaming him.

'Sir, we only tried to help the patient. Baseless allegations are not for encouraging us. This is the fact. He did not die because of our dereliction. Hope that you would believe me. I will be careful about dealing with cases like this.'

Dr Praveen stormed out of the room. He was very unhappy about the developments. He descended the staircase and went to the canteen.

Two weeks had passed since the death of Aishumma. Arumughan was still in the hospital. Urmila was straining at the leash to hit home. Days were dragging on. The warning by the head nurse had hurt her mind. People were observing her. What do they think of her? She does not need their conduct certificate. Why they are so enthusiastic to poke their nose into the affairs of others. She did not like it.

It was afternoon. Urmila was seated near her father's bed. She felt drowsy. She put her head on the bed and slept. Arumughan lay there watching other patients and visitors. Then a visitor came to their bed. Arumughan called his daughter. She rubbed her eyes.

'Who is this?' Arumughan asked her.

Sameer was standing there with a smile. They had never met after Aishumma's death. He was sporting a beard and looked exhausted. On seeing him, her drowsiness vanished. Her face became bright.

'How is your father?' he asked.

She invited him to take a seat. Arumughan stared at the stranger.

'He is the son of the mother who was with you in the ICU,' she explained.

'How is your mother?' Arumughan asked.

Suddenly, Sameer was lost in thought. Many events flashed through him. He said nothing.

'Take rest father, speak little,' he said at last and sat there for some time more. Urmila was brimming with happiness inside. She wanted to ask him many things. Language failed her. What to ask and where to begin? She did not know.

'Are all the funeral rites over?' she asked after a long spell of silence.

'Oh yes. Let me go back.' he stood up and walked out. She followed him across the ward.

'Shall we have a cup of tea?' he asked.

'Let me tell my father and come back to join you', she darted to her father.

* * *

Chapter 13

AT noon, the head nurse Santhakumari came running to the ICU. She conspired something with Sr Jessie and both went to the ward. Dr Praveen was in the ICU. They did not tell him anything. He was scrutinising the first print of his thesis. There were typing errors. Two days had passed since he began the corrections. It had to be finished fast. After that, the final print was to be taken. It was to be endorsed by the guide. So much work was left.

The patients were dosing off. The beep sound of the cardiac monitor and the humming of the ceiling fan together created a peculiar sound in the ICU. All the patients were in stable condition. It was a relaxed day. Hence, he could get enough time to read and correct.

Head Nurse Santhakumari and Sr Jessie came to him.

'Did you know, doctor?' the head nurse asked.

'What?' he lifted his head.

'Something is wrong with Varghese,' Santhakumari said. He arched his brows and looked at Santhakumari.

'I shall tell him properly. You may go home as your duty is over,' Sr Jessie said.

Santhakumari went to her changing room.

Varghese had come to the ICU after a heart attack two weeks back. Later, he was transferred to the ward. He had no relatives with him. One of his friends was assisting him.

Long back, Varghese was a famous journalist based in Delhi. He was a columnist in some of the English dailies. He had been living a high-profile life. High income and good connections propelled him into alcoholism.

In the meantime, he became intimate with a Kerala girl employed in a private company. Later, he married her. Life was good in the beginning. But excessive alcoholism sowed the seeds of discord in conjugal life. He would stay away from home for weeks together. His wife advised him and tolerated him a great deal. But he could not change.

Days came to pass. She became friendly with many others. When he came to know about it, they quarrelled and it ended up in their separation.

Varghese lost his job. For many years, he lived alone in his small house in Delhi. Then he came back to Kerala.

His family members did not welcome him. He did odd jobs. Many more years slipped away. Now he is forty-five. A friend brought him to the hospital because of chest pain. He was in the ICU for one week. Once he was transferred to the ward, a woman came to look after him.

When questioned, he admitted she was his ex-wife. She has been taking care of him all these days. She was always with him. Varghese was thrilled. He was even oblivious to his illness. After all, she had come looking for him in his misfortune. He contemplated a great deal about the vicissitudes of life. Her presence was paradise to him.

Santhakumari had been observing her and many suspicions cropped up. Sister did not like her style. She had been meddling up with the matters of others and was very talkative. Not only that, in the corridor to the latrine, she was seen in a compromising position with a police constable who was accompanying a prisoner.

This was reported by nursing assistant Chandran. The head nurse informed the unit chief. Varghese was going to be discharged. But this afternoon she vanished. Varghese is not disturbed by her disappearance, but she had coaxed him to sign some papers about the ownership of his house in Delhi.

Varghese rolled on his bed and burst into tears. He was going insane. He cursed her. 'Traitor, you cheated me on my deathbed.' He hated the entire world. Sr Jessie and the head nurse had gone to the ward to watch his hysteria.

All bystanders gathered around Varghese. They understood nothing. Sisters told them the story. They consoled him; some others softly massaged his arms. Some massaged his back. Still, Varghese could not control himself.

Arumughan closed his eyes and lay in his bed. The disturbance in the ward did not affect him. Then Sameer appeared in the ward. Seeing him, Urmila got up and went to him. They spoke something and went out.

She thought her father was asleep. But he had seen them. Tears rolled down his cheeks. Sameer took her to his friend's ice cream parlour close to the hospital. On that day, Urmila came very late to the ward. Arumughan did not ask her anything.

* * *

Chapter 14

ARUMUGHAN felt much better. He needed no more injections. The medicines were working on him. The doctor was thinking of discharging him. On that day, the chief and Dr Naushad came for the rounds. When they came to Arumughan, he was sitting on the bed.

'How are you?' the chief asked.

'Please let me go home,' he said.

Chief put the stethoscope on his chest.

'BP is stable, sir,' Dr Naushad said. The chief checked the latest ECG. Then he looked at Arumughan and Urmila.

'You may go home. But don't stop the medication. Don't strain and please take rest.'

Arumughan nodded happily. The chief moved to the next bed.

When he was in the women's ward, Dr Naushad discussed Rema's case with him.

'I think she may be put inside,' the chief said.

'We will do it right now, sir,' Dr Naushad gave instructions to the sister.

Rema was having breathing trouble. Her face and hands were swollen. She was struggling to breathe.

Damu's mother could not understand what the doctors were saying and discussing. She blinked and mumbled something.

Shortly Rema was transferred to the ICU. She was panic-stricken and sweating. Sister fixed ECG leads and connected them to the monitor. Dr Naushad was surprised by the ECG graph. The graph was erratic.

Damu and his mother waited outside. Damu had taken care of her earnestly. He had an immaculate love for her. He had been taking care of her from the first night of the wedding to this day. She was concerned about that. She could never return his love for her. Why was god like that?

But Damu's mother had a different mindset. She did not appreciate her son pampering the girl. She believed Rema was sick from childhood and that it was concealed from them. Sometimes she would even tell this to Rema's face. Damu's mother would share her frustration with the sisters. Rema had been sick for a long time. I am worried about my son. He supported her by doing manual labour. He married her because he loved her and what happened? His wages are not enough for her medicines. When I see my son's drudgery, it pains my heart. It is his fate. What else can

I say? If this ends somehow, he could marry another girl and my son would be happy, at least for a day.

'Don't say like that. She will be cured,' they would tell the woman, though they knew it was not the truth.

Arumughan was discharged in the afternoon. Urmila received the discharge card. Salgunan also was there. When Salgunan was gone to call a taxi, the sister called Urmila aside.

'Give medicines to your father punctually. Do you go out for work?'

'No, there is nobody at home to manage everything.'

'It is okay. But don't think I am sermonising. Take me as your elder sister. Why do you hang around that Muslim boy? People will spread rumours.'

Urmila said nothing. Her face became morose. There was moisture in her eyes. She could say nothing.

'No, don't cry here. Wipe your eyes and go to the ward.'

When Urmila was going out, Dr Praveen came to the ICU. When she saw him, Urmila bent her head and walked towards the ward.

'Arumughan has been discharged, isn't it, sister?' he asked.

'Yes.'

'Then why is his daughter crying? She should be happy that they are going home.'

'It is a different story, doctor. Petty matter.'

Sr Jessie told him what was happening between her and Sameer and the head nurse's intervention.

'Then there is another development doctor. The so-called ex-wife of Varghese and that police officer were seen together in town. She is a clever woman. That police constable is playing the fool.'

'He may be cleverer than her,' the doctor smiled.

Salgunan parked the car outside and came up to collect the bags and other things of Arumughan. A nursing assistant took him in the wheelchair to the parking lot. Urmila walked behind them. Arumughan was lost in thought. He forgot about his illness. The energy was filling him. Sometime back, a proposal had come for Urmila. Tomorrow he would enquire into that Urmila must be married at the earliest. He made plans in silence.

* * *

Chapter 15

DR. Praveen and Dr Naushad were going to finish their course after that month. Their theses were ready. The guide had approved of them. Two more months were left for the university examination. Copies of the thesis had to be sent to the university. It could be sent only with the signature of the professor and the guide. The thesis of Dr Naushad was a difficult one. He had taken an unusual topic, trusting the promise that sufficient cases would be arranged for the study. But the department did not support him adequately. He had to struggle a great deal to ensure enough cases to substantiate his thesis. His endeavour was at last successful. When the thesis was excellent, everybody in the department claimed party to it. They claimed that their support helped him to make it.

Dr Praveen thought about his plan. He wanted to join a private hospital in his town. His parents were government servants. They wanted him to follow the suit. His wife also was a doctor.

The parents of Dr Naushad are in the Gulf. He was a day scholar, as his house was close to the hospital. He has a wife and two kids. He would migrate with his family to the Gulf once the course was over. Both of them had enjoyed their three years long academic life in medical college. Though study and duty were difficult, they had enjoyed the hospital milieu, especially the services of the head nurse Santhakumari, Sr. Omana, Sr. Jessie and Vilasini. Vilasini was like a history book. During the free hours, she would narrate the old things like a parrot. Also, she efficiently handled the official matters of the PG trainees. Everybody knew she could do it all perfectly. Her arrival at the door of the ICU had been quite impressive. She appeared more regal and authentic than the professor himself.

Sr. Santhakumari was always particular to keep the seminar hall and the classrooms of the PG trainees spic and span. The sisters arranged everything for the doctors in the ward. There were no lapses from their side.

After lunch, Dr Praveen went to the ICU. Sr. Jessie was copying the prescriptions from the case sheet.

'Have you had lunch?' she asked.

'Yes, just now. There was too much rush in the OP today. I could not attend the new admissions in the ward. Has the ICU been peaceful?'

'There is no complicated case in the ICU now that Aishumma is no more.' She handed over the case sheets to the doctor.

'Sister, we are about to finish our course.'

'When you are all gone, you will leave behind an emptiness here.'

'Not like that. In the government sector, nobody is permanent and forever. When one goes, another comes. When we are gone, another batch will come. The show will continue. When cured patients go, new patients come.'

'Are you going to settle in your town?'

'Nothing is certain. I will look for hospitals after the university exam. Some hospitals have invited me. I have promised nothing. First things first,' he said.

'We had good solidarity here. Every parting is painful. Time will heal every wound. Time will flush out everything.'

Her words were faltering. She wiped her eyes with a towel from the pocket and rubbed her face.

'Sister, you are becoming sentimental. Take nothing seriously. Deep attachments result in deep pain. Nothing happens in the mind deliberately. The chemistries of certain people click. Friendships coalesce and develop depending upon the chemistries. This is not a conscious and purposeful process. And then partings become pernicious.'

'It was classic. You are more philosophical than expected. It is wonderful that you could take things on a philosophical plain.'

The telephone in the ICU rang. Sister attended to the phone.

'Doctor, there is an emergency case in Ward Number 30. They are requesting your help,' she told him.

Dr Praveen took his bag and stethoscope and went out immediately to perform his exigent duty.

* * *

Chapter 16

IN the evening, Dr Praveen went to the library to go through the journals. He prepared notes on some new studies found in the journal. They will be useful in the exam, especially in the viva voce. Then he walked to the hostel across the campus. His mind was crowded with thoughts. He brooded on the further preparations needed for the forthcoming examination; the portions left to be read and many other things flashed through his mind. Many people coming in the opposite direction smiled at him and he smiled back. When he was about five minutes away from the hostel, his cell phone rang and he picked it. The call was apparently from the neighbourhood.

'Hello, Dr Praveen I am Sr. Jessie.'

'What happened sister, where are you?'

'I am at home. I am not feeling well. I have a headache. Hence I am on leave for two days,' her sound was broken. He assumed that something was wrong with her.

'Did you take medicines?' he asked.

'Yes, doctor. But I have some other problems. I want to ask you one thing,' she paused.

'What do you want to know? Tell me,' he encouraged.

'Could you kindly come to my house tomorrow? I shall tell you the route. My husband also will be here. Please come in the afternoon when you are free.'

'It is all right. Please tell me the route. I will come in the afternoon,' he promised her.

Sister told him about the route to her house. He went to his room and changed. Then he took a book and read. But he could not concentrate. He wondered what was bothering the sister. Tomorrow he might know it all. He should wait. After dinner, he called home. His wife and child were doing well. He was exhausted when he reached his room.

He saw Sr Jessie in a bed. Her head was supported by two pillows and she seemed to have a severe headache. She was in an apathetic condition and could not speak. Both her hands were pressing her forehead. She would weep and stare at the whirring ceiling fan and jerk her head. He wondered what was wrong with her. She said nothing. He called out to her. Suddenly, everything was blank, and he wondered where he was. He was in his hostel room and it was only a dream.

He put on the light and drank water from the bottle. It was only two-thirty in the morning. He put out the light and went to sleep again.

Dr Praveen left the hospital after 3 p.m. the next day. It was easy to find Jessie's house. Palace Road was to the right of the head office of a famous daily in the city. Her house was the second one behind Amruta DTP Centre on Palace Road. It was a cute little house. There was a garden in front with different roses. There were butterflies and dragonflies all over. When he opened the gate, she appeared at the windowsill. By the time he reached the front door, she had opened it. She had put on a light blue churidar. She invited him to the house and offered him a seat on the sofa.

He watched Jessie. Her hair was in disarray. She looked weak and her eyes had lost their natural sheen. She stood in front of him.

'What happened sister, where is your husband?' he asked.

She said nothing for some time. Then she went inside. He sat on the sofa and observed the room. There were many beautiful dolls and toys in the room. In the corner, cute garments for kids were arranged. He found those garments familiar. Somewhere he had seen those garments. Yes, he had got a dozen of them on the day of his child's christening day. So it was Sr

Jessie who sent it anonymously, and she had never mentioned it.

Jessie appeared again with tea and sweetmeat. He was still seated there.

'Have tea,' she offered.

'Sister, tea can wait. I came here because you are not feeling well.'

She forced him to have tea. He slurped up the vanilla flavoured tea. Her behaviour was strange. She was not like this in the hospital. He put the teacup on the tray. She stood there watching it.

'Doctor, please scold me, please be angry with me,' she exploded.

He was taken aback by her sudden change of mood.

'Sister, please tell me what is wrong with you.'

Her eyes became red. Her face was like clouded heavens.

'I wanted to talk to you alone. That is why I invited you here so that I could have you entirely to me. It was a lie when I told you that my husband would be here. He is gone home for a week in connection with his mother's cataract surgery. I was sick in mind. I lost my peace of mind when you told me you were all going away after the course. You have a special place in my mind. I know I am married. I know that you have a wife and child. Still, I fancy you are somebody dear to me. Maybe it is because of my frailty. But I cannot forget you. I am being ravaged and tormented by wild thoughts. I am feeling lonely without my husband. Then I wanted to talk to you. I know it is wrong. But I cannot help it. Please scold me, please be angry with me. Please tell me I am wrong and degraded,' she blurred off.

Dr Praveen got angry in the beginning. Then he realised that anger was not a solution. The situation had to be tackled delicately. He had not expected this kind of behaviour.

'Sister, don't take this seriously. We have a unique existence, we have different paths. We met, became acquaintances and worked together. That was the end. We both know that there is nothing more to it. Then why should you be miserable?'

She was not listening to him.

'Dr Praveen, please don't justify me. Criticise me and say that I was wrong. I invited you here because of my selfishness. Please scold me and say that my mistakes are my mistakes.'

He felt like laughing. Still, he controlled himself.

'Sister, everybody makes petty minor mistakes. You may correct yourself. But please don't pull others into it. After a few days, you will be sorry for what you said. Hence forget it all and join for duty tomorrow.'

Jessie cried. He allowed her to cry. It had a therapeutic effect; it might ease out the pressures inside. He sat there silently watching the toys and dolls. She sat on the floor and sobbed violently.

He consulted his watch; it was time to go. She wiped her eyes and got up.

'Sister, let me go. Forget everything. Nothing happened.'

He walked out. The plant in the garden swayed gracefully in the sweeping breeze.

'I forgot to tell you one thing. Those little garments you sent were beautiful.'

When he referred to the garments, a faint simper flitted on her lips. She stood there watching him disappearing behind the gate.

* * *

Chapter 17

EVERY month, Arumughan was taken to the hospital for follow up. Urmila was always with him. Doctor asked him not to stop the medicines. His heartbeat was normal. He was advised not to strain much and to come back after six weeks.

On the way to the hospital, Urmila would meet Sameer. She would inform him on the phone in advance about the date of their visit. When her father would wait for his turn in the OP section, she would sneak away for her cherished liaison with Sameer. Either they would go to a deserted place or the canteen. Sameer would tell her about his plans and business prospects. His brothers were prevailing on him to go with them to the Gulf. But he wanted to stay back. In the beginning, his mother was his justification to stay at home. Now that she is no more their pressure on his has mounted. They say that his business has no future in the country. Still, he did not want to leave. Urmila was one factor that held him back.

She was thrilled to hear that. She felt she was an important entity in another person's life. He was controlling his future. It implies that he loves her so much. How fast changes happen in life. She was like a desiccated tree in the in the desert and he was like a cool breeze. Her branches were softly dancing in the breeze. The breeze offered a heady ecstasy. New buds were coming up. The hospital joined them. Circumstances were the architects of experiences, she thought.

Recently, two marriage proposals had come for her. One proposal did not proceed, and the boy backed out. The second one seemed plausible enough to Arumughan and Salgunan. But she refused to have a marriage. She insisted she was too young for that. She wanted to be with her brother and father for some more years.

'I may cease to be today or tomorrow. I want to see you settled in life before I fade away.'

'Then what about my brother,' she asked.

'He is a man. Daughters are different. You don't know the mind of a parent,' he said.

'I don't need a marriage now. Kindly find a bride for Salgunan.'

He felt miserable by her attitude. He had some suspicions. But he did not ask her anything. He kept everything to himself.

Arumughan's treatment was expensive. Salgunan managed it somehow. In addition, Urmila had taken up a tailoring job to support the domestic economy.

Elsie from Kunnuparambu was disposing of her sewing machine. Urmila went to her to inspect the machine. A tumour had developed in the lower part of her knee. Hence doctors asked Elsie to stop using the machine, and she had to have surgery. That was the reason for selling away the machine that was not very old or overused. She said that she would get back to Elsie after discussing with her brother Salgunan.

On the way back from Elsie, she contacted Sameer on his cell phone. He asked her to come to the city on the following Wednesday. He offered to go for a movie and to sit for some time in the park. He asked her to tell her father that she was going to a girlfriend of hers in the city. She was excited by his invitation. Happiness rippled through her mind. She offered to come as asked. She wanted to tell him about the proposals. Also that she may not resist the proposals for long.

Rema felt a little better in the ICU. She was breathing better. There was no swelling on her limbs and face. For how long? She could eat food as well. Damu, who toiled day in and day out for her welfare, waited outside. He fondly hoped that God would answer his prayers. But his mother had fresh ideas. She expected Rema to die, eventually.

When Dr Praveen was examining Rema, Sr Jessie came to the ICU.

'Good afternoon,' she wished him. Her duty was to begin at midday. Dr Praveen wanted to discuss certain matters with her. He felt she was distancing herself from him. Was it because of his advice? Her standoff was disturbing him. Also, he felt he was chasing her away. Sister dropped her bag in her room and came back.

'Are you a busy doctor?

'Not much, all patients are stable,' he sat at his table.

'Have you had lunch,' she asked.

'Not yet.'

'Then have lunch. I will take care of everything in the meantime,' she offered.

Sr Jessie examined the case sheets and loaded the syringe.

He went out for lunch. When he returned, Vilasini was in the ICU.

'Doctor, I was informed from the office that your thesis has been forwarded to the university. You can wait for the examination date,' Vilasini told him. He sat near her.

Vilasini stared at him.

'I am tensed a bit,' he confessed. Sr Jessie was also listening to him.

'What is the matter? Is it the forthcoming examination? Don't worry, you will get through. Anxiety will only muddle up your brain,' she consoled him.

'When do you go back home?' he asked.

'What is the matter?' she asked.

'Nothing,' he pulled out a hundred rupee note from the purse and asked nursing assistant Narayanan to bring tea and snacks for all. Narayanan took the money and went out.

The phone in the ICU rang, Vilasini attended the phone. Different emotions flashed through Vilasini's face. Sr Jessie and the doctor watched it with some curiosity. After hanging up, she said, 'Dr Prasad of the chest department has been admitted to the ICU. He is in a critical condition.'

'Is it K.K. Prasad sir?'

'Yes, I am going there. I cannot wait for your tea.'

* * *

Chapter 18

DR. K.K. Prasad passed away in the chest department of the medical college. He had chest problems for a long time. During the past few months, it had exacerbated, and he had gone on leave. Very few had known that he was mortally sick. Even though he was on leave, every week he used to take classes for PG students.

Some thought that he should be taken abroad for advanced treatment. But Dr Prasad did not agree with that. He knew how long he would live. He knew more than anybody else that medical science cannot do much for him. He was a good medical teacher, a noted young scientist and the youngest member of the medical council. He was only forty-five. Within a short period, he had made a name as an excellent doctor. A wide range of people was under his treatment. All of them deeply loved him and respected him.

The entire institution slipped into a spell of sadness after his death. In the beginning, nobody believed that he was no more. His body was brought to the portico of the hospital. People from many sections of the society flowed in to pay their last respects for the departed soul, after that the body was taken to his hometown, Vadakara.

A condolence meeting was held in the medical college. Doctors, students, staff and his friends spoke on the occasion. Dr Praveen also took part in the meeting. When different people remembered him, Vilasini was on the verge of tears.

Two months had passed. Arumughan was more or less stable. He wanted to find a groom for his daughter, Urmila. Salgunan also needed a life partner.

When each proposal came, Urmila's mind hoped that Sameer would come to her house one day. How will her father react? They will not easily reconcile to that prospect. As he is a Muslim, her people may not approve of that. There will be problems in Sameer's family as well. She thought about the possibility of forgetting him. But it was impossible to forget Sameer. He is staying back only for her sake.

On that day before Arumughan's next journey to the hospital, she called Sameer from a telephone booth. He was not available. The computer told her that the phone was switched off. She was disappointed.

While returning from the cardiology OP, her earnest eyes looked at him everywhere. No, he was not there. She was shattered. Arumughan wondered why she was so gloomy.

At night Urmila couldn't sleep. She called him again. He will not go far away. Usually, he is immediately available on the cell phone. She stared into the thick mystery of darkness. Slumber came to her very late.

The next day, while going to the grocer, she called him again from the booth. She tried many times. The phone was switched off. At last, she took the risk of calling him on the land phone. She traced out his number from a small pocket diary. Fortunately, the bell rang on the other side.

'Hello,' a female sound answered her.

'Can I speak to Mr Sameer?'

'Who is speaking?'

'I am Urmila, his friend.'

'I am his sister; you are his classmate at school, aren't you? He has told me about you. He went abroad exactly one month back. He got a good placement there. His marriage will be in three months. She is a beautiful girl from Thiroorangadi. He had asked me to tell you these things when you call. He will invite you to the marriage. In case he forgets, I invite you in advance. Good morning. I am hanging up.'

The phone went dead. Was it a fantasy or truth? Urmila was buckling. Her head was whirling. Earth appeared to be turning upside down. Sameer is gone without telling her anything. He is gone far and away. She remembered the things he had told her at the cinema.

'One of these days, I will come to your house to meet your father and seek your hand. Even if they are all dead against it, I will call you and you must come away with me.'

After all that rapturous promise, he has ditched her. After the movie, back in the ice cream parlour, he had kissed her hand and emphasised his promise, and on the very next day, he was gone without a word. Oh God, this cannot be true!

With tearful eyes, she gave money to the telephone booth and went away. She was not herself anymore. When she reached home, she could not sleep at night. She was shivering. Salgunan gave her a Paracetamol 500mg tablet and applied balm on her forehead.

'Tomorrow we will go to the health centre. These days fever can be dangerous,' he said. Her mind was in the throes of acute pain. Darkness spread before her eyes, portending evil things. She had nightmares. Then she wept silently. Her pillow became wet with her tears. The next morning, Salgunan forcefully took her with him.

'I will take you to the health centre. You can come back with the medicines,' he said.

The health centre was crowded. The doctor prescribed two types of medicines. Some free medicine was provided by the health centre. Then Salgunan went for the job.

On the way back, Urmila tried Sameer's number once again. Again, she got information that the phone was switched off.

* * *

Chapter 19

ONE more heart stopped beating in the ICU. It was Rema's. Doctors were expecting this. But they were not prepared for that on that day because she had improved a great deal during the past few days. She had been more pleasant and her words reflected on it. Now her dramatic exit saddened them all.

Things went topsy-turvy in the morning. Her heartbeat abruptly shot up. Unusual graphs appeared on the cardiac monitor. She had chest pain and her head was spinning. Then her BP plummeted and her memory was gone. Dr Sooraj, who was on duty, gave her some injections. Shock treatment was given thrice but to no avail.

Her life ended within the four walls of the ICU. Damu cried aloud hearing that. His life had reached a crossroads.

Even after two days, Urmila continued to be sick. Even though the fever had subsided, her head was heavy and her limbs did not have the strength to support her. On the second day, Salgunan did not go for the job. He did all the cooking, and he prepared a medicinal porridge with broken rice. Arumughan also was disappointed by her condition.

'She is sick because she had been suffering for me in the hospital for long.' He lamented.

'No, father, the doctor says that this is viral fever. This will subside with proper rest,' Salgunan told his father.

In the meantime, bedridden, Urmila was sinking into the unfathomed depths of agony. Sameer is gone without a word. What was between him and her? Was it love or an ineffable affinity?

She remembered the days in the hospital. Almost every evening, he was with her to the canteen. Did that result in an emotional attachment? His presence had indeed made her light-headed and happy.

But had she induced the same feelings in him? Or was it just beastly lust? In what capacity had he touched her and told her he loved her? Was it because of that attachment that he had taken her to the ice cream parlour outside the hospital? Was he loving her or pretending? She could not understand. She remembered how he embraced her and whispered in her ear: 'I love you, I like you' and it was when the power supply was gone in the hospital corridor. She remembered how he fondled her and kissed her cheeks and lips in the ice cream parlour. Did he love her? He was not loving her, he was cheating on her. Why Sameer did that to her? He assaulted her modesty and got away with it, taking advantage of her goodwill and inexperience.

Head nurse Santhakumari and Sr. Jessie had forewarned her. When they did that, it had been revolting to her. They were unwelcome intruders. And now she is all alone. What was their motivation to advise her? Were they doing that from their own experiences, probably? Sister Santhakumari could foresee the shape of things to come. But now Urmila was haunted by hundreds of thousands of thoughts. Her mind and body were giving in. Her body was steaming.

She had none to confide in. How can she possibly tell her father and brother the reason for her illness? Even if she does that, how they are going to react? Her father may look down upon her. Her image may collapse in their minds. She dreaded that situation. Darkness surrounded her. She was devouring darkness. Darkness taught her that reality fades in darkness. That darkness is better. She wanted to dive into the bottomless depths of darkness. How could she do that?

She could not resist when Sameer touched her and kissed her. She had taken his words for their face value. He had exploited that trust. Now he is gone, leaving her in the lurch. She has been left alone in the world as a cheap woman, a fallen woman. No Sameer, my dignity and integrity will never be compromised. I will never live like that. I will defeat you. I have decided. I can foresee your failure, your headlong fall. She was thinking incoherently.

At night, when everybody was asleep, she got up. Then she cried silently. She went to her father's room and stood there looking at him. All people will blame her father for giving birth to a cheap woman.

She crossed Salgunan's room and went to the atrium and then to the kitchen. She opened the kitchen door and went out. There was a thin moonlight, and the night was calm. Stars twinkled. With hazy eyes, she went to the well. Down in the well, she saw the crescent moon smiling at her. It was beckoning and smiling at her.

* * *

Chapter 20

SR JESSIE was on long leave. She was preparing for the journey abroad. Some documents of her long leave had to be submitted at the office. Head Nurse Santhakumari and Vilasini did that. The office was satisfied with the documents.

Santhakumari was worried about how to manage the ICU in the absence of Jessie. When they crossed the casualty, Santhakumari invited Vilasini to the canteen. Vilasini declined the invitation and went back. Trollies and wheelchairs were rolling up and down the corridor with patients. Some patients were being transferred to the wards, some were being taken to the x-ray units. The trolleys were shadowed by the relatives of the patients.

In the casualty, there was a crowd in the corner. The bed was screened by a green curtain. With a curiosity natural to human beings, Vilasini looked into the bed. It was a familiar face, a girl. Vilasini wracked her brain, somewhere she had seen her. She was seen in the cardiology ward. But who could she be?

Vilasini went to the nursing station. The sisters greeted her lovingly.

'The girl seems familiar to me. What is her name? Where is she from?' Vilasini asked.

'She is dead already. It is said that she fell into a well. Her name is Urmila. Nobody knows what happened. A beautiful girl indeed, homely and sweet. Do you know her?'

When she heard the name, Vilasini was stunned. She was a bystander of a patient in the ICU. She strained to remember the girl.

Urmila's body was brought for post mortem. The news spread like wildfire. People fabricated many stories. Nobody knew the truth.

'She was at an inflammable age. Maybe some failed love.'

'She was a good girl. What to say. People are the victims of their thoughts. Even God cannot change it.'

'She must have been worried that no marriage proposal was getting through.'

'Probably she had a secret relationship when she was in the family way he might have ditched her. That explains everything.'

Arumughan's family was in shambles. Everybody was silent. Arumughan spread himself on the floor. Salgunan stood outside the mortuary like a disoriented man. His friends and neighbours were with him. Post

Mortem was over by three o'clock. A sea of people had gathered at his house when the ambulance arrived. Urmila's sisters broke down when they saw her dead. Arumughan sat in a corner. People came and went.

A grave was dug on the southern side. People were hurrying to bury her. The ambulance went back.

It was all over by ten o'clock at night. The relatives went back after that one by one. Arumughan's daughters, their husbands, their children and Salgunan remained. Nobody said anything. They understood nothing. It was a puzzle. Salgunan suppressed his anguish. Late at night, they slept scattered here and there. The next day, all except the eldest daughter went back. Salgunan did not come out of the house for four days. He found emptiness in front of him. His mind was heavy. One day, his employer came and consoled him. On the fifth day, his elder sister's husband came intoxicated. He quarrelled with his wife.

'Early in the morning, we should leave this bloody place. Your youngest sister was a slut. She killed herself for a reason. She was freaking out with a Muslim. It was an affront on us, an affront on our self-esteem.'

Salgunan and Arumughan were petrified. They could say nothing. At a later stage, Salgunan asked the drunkard to shut his mouth. Still, he kept on insulting them. His wife was weeping helplessly. After midnight, he fell asleep.

The next morning, the husband and wife went back. Salgunan and Arumughan were left behind. Salgunan had no thirst for life. Why did she do that? Did she make any mistakes as alleged? No, never. She is his innocent and immaculate little sister. She can never be impure. People are telling lies and spreading canards. He consoled himself.

That evening, one of Salgunan's friends visited him. He let him know that there was some truth in the rumour. There cannot be smoke without a little fire.

Salgunan's inner tension increased. That day he walked out of the house after many days. He had no destination, and he did not come back.

The next day, Arumughan went out in search of his son. On the footpath, he was stuck in chest pain. Then he collapsed. His neighbours lifted him and brought him back to the house. He was sweating; he could not speak. People searched for Salgunan. He was nowhere. The neighbours were confused. They decided, at last, to take Arumughan to the hospital. Otherwise, the old man will die, they reasoned.

Arumughan was taken to the medical college. After ECG and emergency medication, he was transferred to the cardiology ICU.

Head nurse Santhakumari was there when his trolley stopped in front of the ICU on the first floor. Immediately, she recognised him. She quickly opened the door to admit him.

Bed number five was vacant. ECG leads were fixed and connected to the monitor. Injections were given. But Arumughan was unconscious.

Dr Sooraj was on duty in the ICU. Dr Praveen and Dr Naushad had already left the hospital. Sr Jessie having passed the test and was in Madras as a prelude to her exodus to the US. She had sent a message to Dr Praveen: 'I will call you on 14th February.'

Dr Sooraj asked Sr Nirupama to give an injection.

'That injection is not here, doctor,' she said.

'Then ask them to buy it quickly.'

'He always has a girl with him. She must wait outside. Give her this prescription,' said sister Santhakumari.

No girl was waiting outside. Still, somebody took the prescription and brought the injection shortly.

Sister loaded the injection and watched the monitor.

The medicine was working on the patient.

The graph of the monitor was becoming normal. Doctor and sister watched him. He regained his consciousness after half an hour.

Arumughan opened his eyes and looked around. He saw the pale blue walls, which were familiar. Hospital again, who brought him here? He looked at the doctor and sister. Dr Sooraj was satisfied. He went to his table and wrote on the case sheet. Arumughan became lucid. His eyes became wet.

'Why I do not die. I cannot live anymore,' he told himself, and the walls looked at him. His tears rolled down.

The clock on the wall had stopped long ago!

* * *

Dr P. Sajeevkumar

Dr P. Sajeevkumar is the son of late Palissery Venugopala Menon and Unnikkattil Jayabharathi from Arimpur in Thrissur, Kerala. His school education was at Arimpur and higher education was at Thrissur St. Thomas College, Thrissur Medical College, and Calicut Medical College.

He served for many years at the Chest Hospital of Thrissur Medical College. Currently, he is a Pulmonary Medicine Consultant in the Kerala State Health Department.

He is a literary enthusiast and a writer. His collection of poems in Malayalam was published in 2011. He had composed a music album in Malayalam which was tuned by Vidyadharan master. A book on his experiences as a doctor was published in 2012. The Malayalam version of this novel was published in the Sunday edition of *Janayugam* daily.

Dr Radhika, Associate Professor Thrissur Medical College, is his wife. Children are Nanda Kishore and Soorya Prathap.

Address:

Dr P. Sajeevkumar
'Sarayu'
Athani P.O., Thrissur–680 581
Phone: +91 9846310596
Email: drsajeevkumar@rediffmail.com

www.ingramcontent.com/pod-product-compliance
Lightning Source LLC
Chambersburg PA
CBHW050021170726
48282CB00025B/491
* 9 7 8 9 3 9 0 7 5 9 3 4 7 *